HOW SIX FOUND CHRISTMAS

How Six Found Christmas

written and illustrated
by Trina Schart Hyman

Holiday House / New York

This book was originally published by
Little, Brown & Co. in 1969.

Library of Congress Cataloging-in-Publication Data
Hyman, Trina Schart.
How six found Christmas / Trina Schart Hyman:
illustrated by the author.
p.   cm.
Summary: A little girl's quest for Christmas
leads her into the Great Snow Forest
where she is joined in her search by a cat,
a dog, a hawk, a fox, and a mockingbird.
ISBN 0-8234-0914-7
[1. Christmas—Fiction.]   I. Title.
PZ7.H988Ho   1991   91-70462   CIP   AC
[E]—dc20

For Ed

Once upon a time there was a little girl who had never heard of Christmas and therefore did not know what it was. By chance one day she happened to meet an old wise woman who told her that there was such a thing. But the wise woman did not elaborate on the matter, so the little girl was left as ignorant as before, yet with a great curiosity.

Being a sensible child, she decided that the best way to find out what a Christmas was would be to go and find one, and have a look for herself. So she set out, as many others have done before her, for the Great Snow Forest of the North, to look for Christmas.

She traveled for two days and two nights, and on the morning of the third day she chanced to meet a large gray cat who was sitting at the edge of the forest shaking her paws on account of the snow.

"Where are you going, my child," asked the cat, "and where are your mittens?" This cat was a straightforward, motherly soul.

"I am going to find a Christmas," said the little girl, "and my mittens are in my pocket."

"What on earth is a Christmas?"

asked the cat, astonished. "I have never heard of such a thing. What does it feel like? Is it comfortable and warm? Does it have fur? Is it wet, or dry? Is it cold and sharp and smooth like ice, or is it prickly warm velvet like summer grass? Tell me quickly, for I am curious, being a cat."

"Bless you, Tabby, I don't know what it feels like," answered the child.

"I myself have never felt a Christmas, which is why I am looking for one. If you are really so curious, why don't you come along with me? Then, when I find one, you may feel it for yourself."

To this the cat agreed, and they set off together through the Great Snow Forest. They had not gone far before they met a sad-faced hound, nosing his way from tree to tree.

"I beg your pardon," said the hound, "but did either of you ladies happen to see a rabbit pass this way not long ago?"

"No," said the little girl, "I have seen no rabbit at all. But in your hunting, did you happen to come across a Christmas?"

The dog sat down and gazed at her mournfully. "You know," he said, "I'm not really sure. As a matter of fact, I am not at all sure I know what a Christmas is. What does a Christmas smell like? Is it musty and strong like rabbits and squirrels? Does it smell as delicious and comforting as cooking meat, or as ancient and frightening as old cellars? Does it smell like a human baby, or a river bank, or perhaps like rotting leaves?"

"Bless you, Dog," said the child, "I can't tell you what a Christmas smells like, for I myself have never smelled one. If you are really interested, why don't you come along with us, and when we find a Christmas you may smell for yourself."

Having by now given up the rabbit, the hound decided that this was not such a bad idea, and he fell in step with the cat and the little girl.

They spent the night in a deserted castle, and on the morning of the fourth day the three travelers met a great red hawk perched on the limb of a fir tree.

10

"Halt!" snapped the hawk. Since he was very regal-looking, they all did as they were told. "I have been watching you from afar for a day and a night, and I demand to know where you are going and why you are going there."

"Well of course," said the little girl. "We are looking for a Christmas. It was I who wanted to find one first, you see, because I don't know what it is. And then my friends the cat and the dog decided that they would like to find a Christmas, too. Cat wants to feel it, and Dog wants to smell it. So, although we don't know exactly where we are going, at any rate that is why we are going there."

"I see," said the hawk, frowning and moving from one foot to the other. "Well, I can tell you right now that such a thing does not exist. If it did, I would have seen it on my travels. What does a Christmas look like? Does it glitter? Does it move? Quickly or slowly? Is it dark or bright? What color is it? Is it round and fuzzy or is it flat and clear? Does it change its shape, or does it remain the same?"

"Bless you, Hawk," said the little girl, "I can't answer your questions because I myself have never seen a Christmas, or even heard it described. If you really want to know what it looks like, why don't you come along

with us, and when we find one you may see for yourself."

After a moment's thought, the hawk agreed to come. As the others walked along he flew behind them at a sedate height.

They traveled all that day. Just as evening was coming on they met a wise old fox, who pricked up his ears and grinned when he saw them.

"Whither away?" said the fox, who fancied himself an old-fashioned gentleman.

"Good evening," said the little girl. "We are traveling through the Great Snow Forest, looking for a Christmas. Do you happen to know where we might find one?"

"A Christmas, a Christmas," murmured the fox, looking clever. "No, my dear, I can't say that I know exactly where you could find one at *this* time of year. Perhaps in the summer yes. A *Christmas*, you say? Now let me see....Perhaps I know it by another name. Would you describe the thing for me? What does it taste like? Is there lots of juicy blood? Is it sweet, or salty, or sour, or peppery? Is it crisp? Does it go crunch when one bites it, or does it slip between one's teeth and slide down one's throat? Is it spicy and rich, or is it bland and wholesome?"

"Bless you, old Fox," said the child, "I can't tell you how it tastes, for I have never eaten a Christmas. If you really wish to know all those things, why don't you come along with us? If we find one, you may take a taste. But only a nibble, mind you!"

As the fox was rather hungry, even

a nibble seemed better to him than nothing, so he readily agreed to go along with the others.

The whole of the next day they traveled through the forest, searching for a Christmas. In the late afternoon they met a mockingbird who was amusing himself by pretending he was a nightingale.

"Hullo, hullo!" he said. "What have we here? What brings so many creatures this far into the Great Snow Forest at once?"

"Oh Mockingbird," said the little girl, who was by now getting weary and discouraged, "we are looking for a Christmas. Do you know where we might find one?"

"A Christmas!" exclaimed the Mockingbird, and whistled long and low. "What the devil is that? Tell me what it sounds like, and I'll tell you where to find one. Does it tinkle? Does it shriek? Does it boom and roar, or does it titter and squeak? Does it laugh? Does it sob? Does it use one note, or many? Is it music, or is it noise?"

"Bless you, Mockingbird," said the child, "that I can't tell you, for I have never heard a Christmas. If you wish to know what it sounds like, I advise you to come along with us, for if we ever find one, then you may hear it." And so he did.

And it came to pass that on the

evening of the fifth day they came upon an old green bottle, dropped in the snow by some lonely hunter, perhaps, or a long-dead, frozen king. There it lay, solitary and startling in the Great Snow Forest. And the rays of the setting sun shone on the green glass, and it became as fire and ice, and as the sea and summer.

"Well," said the little girl, "I believe this is possibly what we are looking for. It is certainly very beautiful, and I somehow *feel* that this is a Christmas."

The big gray cat went up to the bottle and put her paw on it. Then she rubbed her whiskers against it, and lay down next to it.

22

"It is smooth and cold," she said. "It has a silky and yet a hard feel to it. Not exactly my cup of tea, but yes, I believe that you are right. This must be a Christmas."

Next the hound went nosing up to the bottle, and sniffed it all over. He put his nose to the opening. Then he looked worriedly at the little girl.

"It smells old," he said. "It smells of past memories, half-forgotten things, both happy and sad. I can't say it smells delicious, but it certainly does have a smell all its own. Musty, sort of. I guess this is what you were looking for."

Then the hawk flew down and perched on the child's shoulder, and

24

gazed at the bottle with his most for-
midable gaze. "Madam," he finally
said, "it is a beautiful object. Pleasing
shape, lovely color, and a sort of inner
fire that gives it a most interesting
glitter. Both round and clear. No real
movement there, of course, but it has
a definite charm nevertheless. I would
say without a doubt that this is a
Christmas, and quite a good example
of one at that."

Now the fox went over and nibbled
at the neck of the bottle. "Certainly
no crunch there, and not any juice,
either," he grumbled. "Tastes of snow,
and winter air, and maybe just a little
salt." He was rather disappointed.
"Yes, I suppose this is a Christmas,

my dear. But if I were you, I'd let it sit until summer. By then it may have gotten some of its flavor back."

The Mockingbird just whispered, "No sound at all. How remarkable! No sound at all!" He shook his head sadly for a while, then he gave a low whistle and flew away.

The little girl took up the bottle, brushed the snow from its sides, and put it under her coat. Then she started on the long journey back home.

The hawk, after expounding a little on the virtues of the Christmas, flew off to the Great Finn Forests to hunt for weasels. The fox, after a day of traveling, thanked the little girl for a pleasant experience, bowed low over her hand, and trotted off to try and get a decent meal somewhere.

The dog and the cat walked her the rest of the way home, and they parted with promises to see one another often, or at least write.

The little girl took the bottle and set it on her table. Then she filled it with branches of red berries, and soft green pine. And the evening stars shone through the window and onto the green glass, making it glisten softly.

And lo! It *was* Christmas!

Christmas is not only
where you find it; it's
what you make of it.